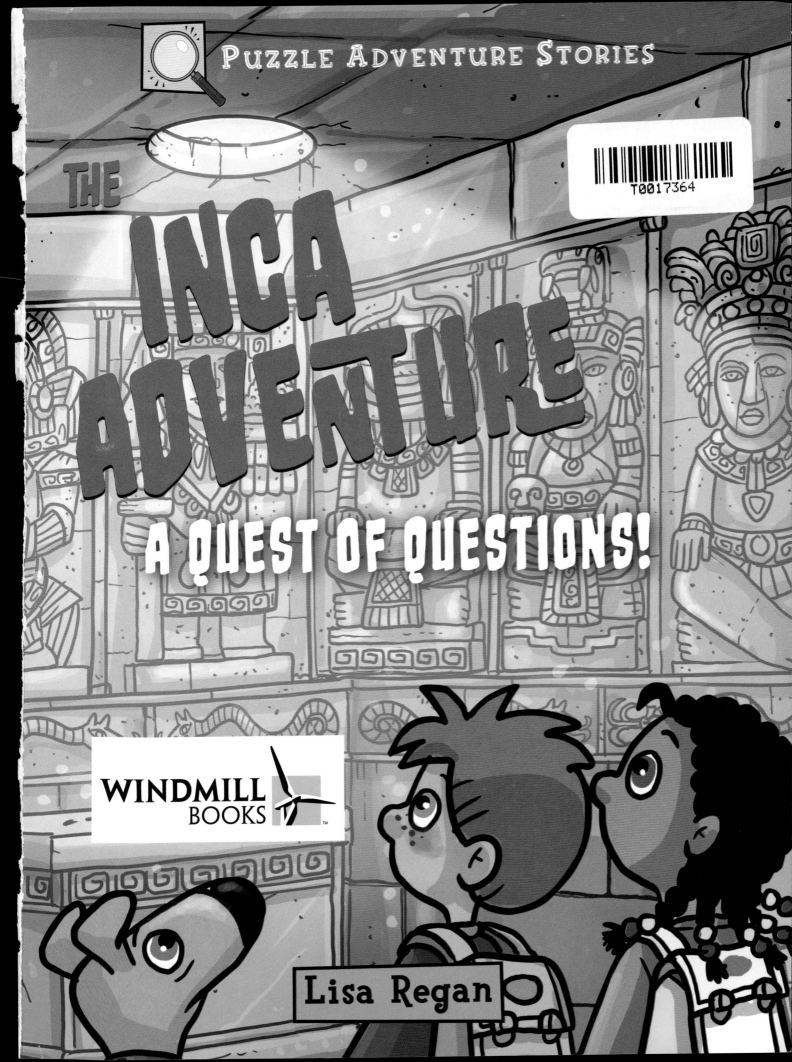

Published in 2019 by **Windmill Books**, an imprint of Rosen Publishing
29 East 21st Street, New York, NY 10010

Written by Lisa Regan
Illustrated by Moreno Chiacchiera
Designed by Paul Oakley, with Emma Randall
Edited by Frances Evans, with Julia Adams

Cataloging-in-Publication Data

Names: Regan, Lisa.
Title: The Inca adventure / Lisa Regan.
Description: New York : Windmill Books, 2019. | Series: Puzzle adventure stories
Identifiers: LCCN ISBN 9781508195467 (pbk.) | ISBN 9781508196303 (library bound) | ISBN 9781508195474 (6 pack)
Subjects: LCSH: Incas--Juvenile fiction. | Peru--Juvenile fiction. | Puzzles--Juvenile fiction.
Classification: LCC PZ7.R443 In 2019 | DDC [E]--dc23

Manufactured in the United States of America

CPSIA Compliance Information: Batch #BS18WM: For Further Information contact Rosen Publishing, New York, New York at 1-800-237-9932

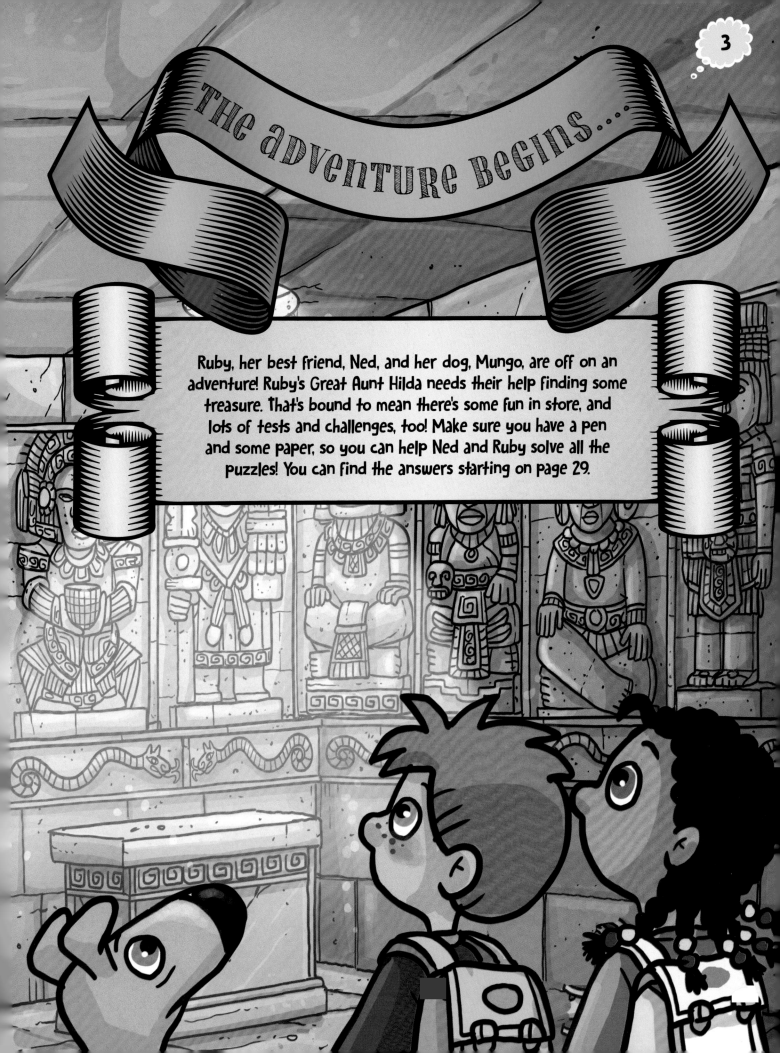

THE ADVENTURE BEGINS....

Ruby, her best friend, Ned, and her dog, Mungo, are off on an adventure! Ruby's Great Aunt Hilda needs their help finding some treasure. That's bound to mean there's some fun in store, and lots of tests and challenges, too! Make sure you have a pen and some paper, so you can help Ned and Ruby solve all the puzzles! You can find the answers starting on page 29.

Where are you?

Ned and Ruby have arranged to meet at the airport, but it's very crowded! Can you spot the two friends and Mungo hidden among all these people?

See if you can find Ruby's adventurous cousin, Nico, too. He's coming along to help the gang... but he'll need waking up!

The secret mission

Ruby calls Ned over and introduces him to Nico. She's very excited! "Great Aunt Hilda has sent me an ancient talisman and this letter," she says, showing them a piece of paper. But it's all in code! Figure out what Hilda wants them to do, using the key below. Write down the answer on your piece of paper.

Dear Ruby and Ned,

Love,
Great Aunt Hilda

CODE KEY

Hmm, what could Hilda mean?

Special delivery

Ruby reaches into her bag and shows the precious item to Ned. "There's a fake one, too," she explains, "for added security." Can you spot nine differences between the two talismans?

 "I can see the differences," says Ned, "but how can you tell which one is real and which one is the fake?" "That's easy," says Nico. "The fake has a little face hidden on it." Did you spot it?

Destination unknown

Ruby doesn't know where they are going, but Hilda has sent her a clue stuck to the back of a map. She shows it to the group. "Hilda says if we find all the hidden words, one will stand out as our destination. Let's see!" Copy all the country names on your piece of paper, and check them off as you find them. Which word is arranged in a different way than all the others?

Ready for takeoff

An announcement asks everyone to check in for the flight to Peru. "That's us!" they yell, and head to the desk. Which check-in desk should they go to?

CLUES:
1. It is divisble by 2.
2. It is also divisible by 3.

Waiting in line

Little do they know, but someone else is after the talisman, too. Dr. Schnurrbart is always chasing after Hilda's treasure, and he's on their tail this time. He has a moustache and red socks. Can you spot him?

Touchdown

Ruby and Ned are so excited! It seems like no time at all before they climb off the plane in Lima and follow Nico from the airport. Hilda has booked them into a hotel for the night. Can you figure out which one it is?

CLUES:
1. It has a blue front door.
2. It has a flag outside.
3. the top floor has a balcony.

And can you guess where Dr. Schnurrbart will be staying?

Special sign

As they check in to their room, the concierge hands Ruby an envelope. "A message for you, Señora." Inside, there is a strange grid, and a note. Their adventure is beginning!

Head for EL POBLADO in the morning! Plot the coordinates on the grid and you will find a special sign. Look for it on the huts when you arrive. Sleep well, H x

(4,8) (5,8) (6,8) (6,7) (7,7) (7,6) (8,6) (8,5) (8,4) (7,4) (7,3) (6,3) (6,2) (5,2) (4,2) (4,3) (3,3) (3,4) (2,4) (2,5) (2,6) (3,6) (3,7) (4,7)

Copy the grid to your piece of paper. Now, plot the coordinates: the first number in a pair shows how many squares to count across. The second number shows how many squares to count up. When you have plotted them all, join them up in the right order. Keep this shape handy, as it will come in useful later!

Taking a trek

The next morning, they set off early and soon leave the city far behind them. Suddenly, their taxi stops. Their driver can't take them any further. Which form of transportation will get them to the correct village?

Off we go!

The kids can't wait to set off, but they squabble about who will lead the llamas. The four llamas that they are going to take on their trek always walk in the same order. Use the clues to figure out which llama goes where.

CLUES:
1. The smallest llama doesn't lead.
2. A llama with red triangles on its saddle goes at the back.
3. The all-white llama follows the leader.
4. A llama with purple triangles on its saddle goes first.

Watch out!

To reach El Poblado, they must trek through a jungle. Nico holds up a hand. "I must warn you about the spiders! Some of them have a nasty bite." How many dangerous spiders are hiding in the trees?

CLUE:
The poisonous spiders have red stripes on them.

Home from home

Soon they see the village through the trees. Figure out which of the huts they should head for (check the shape you drew on your grid earlier) and find a route through the maze to reach it.

Welcome!

There are lots of people outside the hut, and some of them look very important. "We must greet the chief first," Nico whispers. Use the clues to make sure Ned and Ruby show respect to the correct person.

CLUES:
1. He is wearing three necklaces.
2. He has tattoos on both arms.
3. He has a bracelet on his right arm.

Welcome to El Poblado!

Hey there!

Box of rocks

The chief, Mateo, invites the friends inside. He opens a box full of patterned stones and tells them to choose one, so he can be sure that they are carrying the real talisman. Ned whispers to Ruby, "Find one that matches our talisman!" Can you?

Set in stone

Nico is getting fidgety. He uncrosses his legs and sends the box of stones flying across the floor. Oops! But Ned notices something written on the bottom of the box. Can you figure out what it says? Mateo has scribbled down a key to help them figure it out. Write down the answer using your pen and paper.

The missing piece

Before they go to bed, Mateo takes the gang outside and shows them a wall with ancient engravings on it. He tells them that the talisman is part of a bigger item that they must find before they return it to Great Aunt Hilda's friend. Copy the engraving onto a piece of paper. Then use the clues to figure out what they are looking for, and where to find it.

	a	b	c	d
4	R	T	C	A
3	Q	H	L	S
2	E	I	M	Y
1	P	N	D	F

I knew this would come in handy one day!

CLUES:

b3 a2 d4 c1 c1 a4 a2 d3 d3

b2 b1 c4 d4   b4 a2 c2 a1 c3 a2

wake up!

Ned and Ruby wake up bright and early the next day. All the villagers are eager to guide them to the temple, so they hold a competition. The archer with the highest score will show the gang the way. Use the score key to figure out who has won.

Snakes alive!

Their guide packs up some supplies and leads them off through the trees. They are heading for the river... but so is Dr. Schnurrbart! Can you help the friends get to the river safely, avoiding all the snakes (and Dr. S.) on the way? Use your finger to trace a safe path.

River ride

"Looks like the next part of our journey is by boat!" says Ruby. Their guide shows them two canoes and starts putting their supplies inside. The two boats should contain the same supplies. Which item is missing from Boat B?

Jungle safari

As they paddle down the river, the children gasp at all the sights and sounds. "Look! A monkey!" cries Ned. "A toucan!" Ruby points out. "Woof!" barks Mungo, and they are all amazed to see a crocodile slipping into the water. Have some fun spotting wildlife with them.

Can you see these things?
1. A purple butterfly 2. Three green tree frogs 3. A green and orange snake
4. A bear cub 5. A crocodile
6. The stone jaguar

Which way now?

"That's the jaguar stone we saw on the box!" exclaims Ruby. They steer to shore and pack up their bags. Before the guide waves goodbye, he points to different paths into the trees, each with a symbol at the start. "The path that is different from the others will take you to the temple," he explains. Can you spot it?

Trapped!

They make good progress until... WHOOSH! They're trapped! A man with a big moustache appears, rubbing his hands in delight. "Haha! Hilda's clever but she's no match for Dr. P. Schnurrbart, treasure-hunting mastermind extraordinaire! Hand over the talisman, kid."

Which of the ropes should Mungo chew through to set the gang free?
Trace each one with your finger to find out.

The pyramid challenge

"Don't worry, I gave him the fake talisman!" smiles Ruby. They dust themselves off and keep going along the path. They soon emerge into a clearing. "Woah!" gulps Ned. Nico scratches his head. "Do you think the numbers make a pattern?" Copy the numbers on your piece of paper and help them figure it out.

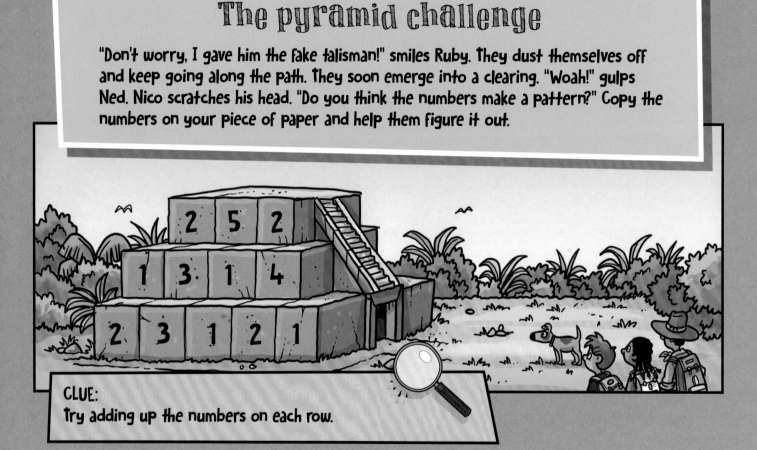

CLUE:
Try adding up the numbers on each row.

Count the blocks

There are lots of doors around the pyramid. "Which do you think is the entrance?" asks Ruby. There are four piles of blocks with compass directons marked next to them outside the temple. Count the blocks in each pile (don't forget to count blocks hidden behind other blocks!). Can you find one that contains the number you found in the puzzle above?

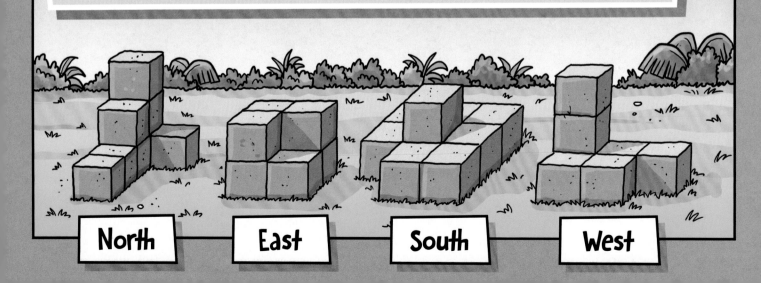

North   **East**   **South**   **West**

Gaining entry

Nico pulls the compass out of his kit, and heads to the entrance on the correct side of the building. The children feel quite awestruck. But which handle should the gang use to open the door? "I think the key is the number 9..." suggests Nico.

CLUE:
Find a zigzag pattern on the door that counts in 9s.

Secrets in the stone

The door opens to reveal a tiny room with no way into the pyramid. What now? There is a wonderful picture on the floor, though. Ned drops to his knees and begins to feel around. "There must be a secret latch somewhere!" he says.

CLUE:
It is hidden in a part that looks like this. Can you find it?

Use your head

A door creaks open to reveal a secret room and... "the headdress!" exclaims Ruby. the talisman fits into it perfectly. Nico gives a whoop of delight, does a little victory dance, and backs into the door, slamming it shut! How are they going to get out now?

CLUE:
Can you spot something hidden in the room that will help them climb out of the hole in the ceiling?

ZigZags

They climb out onto the top of the temple and scramble down a steep flight of stone steps. They need to find Great Aunt Hilda's friend and give them this talisman! Use your finger to trace a way through the ancient ruins and get to the inhabited house at the top of the hill.

Reunited

As they scrabble to the top, a man appears to greet them. "Hilda said it wouldn't take you long. This headdress has been missing from my family's collection for years!" the walls of his museum are covered with headdresses, and Ruby proudly hangs theirs in a space. It completes a set of three. Can you find the other sets in the display?

Nico contacts Hilda to let her know their mission is complete. Her response is short... but intriguing. There's never a peaceful moment in her crazy life!

Talisman returned. Every1 happy. Not bad, huh?!

Gr8! Come home for next mission. H.

Answers

Page 4

Page 5   The letter reads:
I was given this talisman by a friend. Now it must be returned to its owner. Please deliver it safely!

Page 6

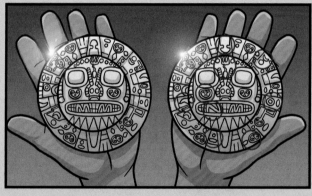

Page 7   Peru is written downward.

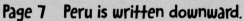

```
Z C H I L E X A B W J U
Y J I L C S A R T N A N
I Y A U G A R A P C F Q
E C U A D O R F E O H M
B O L I V I A E R G A F
H S D K A N A Y U G I O
K S U R I N A M E E D F
P R P A C O L O M B I A
S A L E U Z E N E V M U
L I Z A R B N C B L D L
O D P V J U R U G U A Y
Q L A N I T N E G R A P
```

Page 8   Ready for takeoff: 192
Waiting in line:

Page 9   The children will be staying at Hotel Tía. Dr. Schnurrbart will be staying at Hotel Bigote.

Page 10

Page 11   Llama tours is the only form of transportation that goes to El Poblado.

Page 12   The llamas trek in the following order: Llama D goes first, llama A goes second, llama C goes third, and llama B goes last.

Page 13   there are 6 spiders with red stripes.

Page 14   the kids took this route:

Page 15

Page 16   Box of rocks:

Set in stone: SEEK THE JAGUAR STONE BY THE RIVER

Page 17   HEADDRESS
INCA TEMPLE

Page 18   Archer A has won with a score of 32. Archers B and C have both scored 30.

Page 19

Page 20   A sleeping bag is missing from boat B.

Page 21

Page 22 They need to take path C. That jaguar has three teeth; the rest only have one tooth.

Page 23 Mungo needs to chew through rope A.

Page 24 The pyramid challenge: the numbers on each row, when added up, make 9.

Count the blocks: 9 is the answer to the puzzle above, so the kids need to go to the south side of the pyramid.

Page 25 Gaining entry: the gang should use the fourth handle from the left (9, 18, 27, 36, 45, 54, 63, 72, 81).

Secrets in the stone:

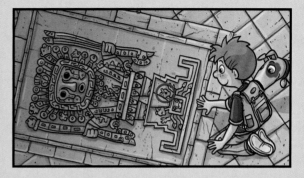

Page 26 There is a rope and a grappling hook hidden on the wall.

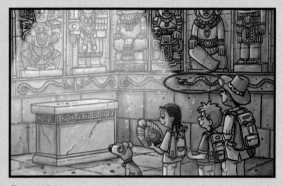

Page 27

Page 28

Glossary

concierge A hotel assistant.

engraving A pattern or picture cut into hard material such as stone or wood.

inhabited When a place or building has someone living in it.

Señora The Spanish word for "Mrs." or "madam."

talisman An object that people believe will bring them luck.

Further Information

Books:

Kamigaki, Hiro. *Pierre The Maze Detective: The Mystery of the Empire Maze Tower*. London, UK: Laurence King, 2017.

Press, Hans Jürgen. *The Black Hand Gang and the Mysterious House*. Bicester, UK: Ravensburger, 2010.

Usborne. *The Usborne Big Book of Puzzle Adventures*. London, UK: Usborne, 2002.

Websites

For web resources related to the subject of this book, go to:
www.windmillbooks.com/weblinks
and select this book's title.

Index

ancient 5, 17, 27

clue 7, 8, 9, 12, 13, 15, 17, 24, 25, 26, 27

code 5

coordinates 10

hut 10, 14, 15

jaguar 21, 22

jungle 13, 21

llama 11, 12

map 7

pyramid 24, 25

Peru 7, 8

river 19, 20, 21

safari 11, 21

South America 7

temple 18, 22, 24, 27